Disney · PIXAR

A Bug's Life

A Berry Brave Troop

Written by

P. Kevin Strader

Illustrated by

Kenny Yamada, Charles Landholm,
and Yakovetic

This book belongs to:

_____

𝒟𝒾𝓈𝓃𝑒𝓎 · PIXAR

A Bug's Life

A Berry Brave Troop

𝒟𝒾𝓈𝓃𝑒𝓎 PRESS

Los Angeles • New York

Adapted from the book originally published by Advance Publishers
© 1998 Disney Enterprises, Inc., and Pixar.

For information address Disney Press, 1200 Grand Central Avenue,
Glendale, California 91201.

ISBN 978-1-368-02797-7
FAC-023680-18211
Printed in China
First Box Set Edition, July 2018
1 3 5 7 9 10 8 6 4 2

For more Disney Press fun, visit www.disneybooks.com
This book was printed on paper created from a sustainable source.

$\mathcal{P}$rincess Dot's Blueberry troop was having its weekly meeting.

Just then, Dot's friend Flik stopped by. He was a grown-up, but he and the little princess got along famously.

"If you want excitement," Flik said, "just start with a new idea!"

Dot smiled. "I know! Let's go camping at Clover Hill," she suggested.

But they needed the Queen's permission.

The Queen thought the Blueberries were too young to go camping by themselves.

"We'll bring Aphie," Dot suggested, pointing to her mother's pet.

"I'm afraid that's not enough," the Queen told her daughter.

"I'll go with them!" Flik volunteered.

The Queen hesitated. Flik's big ideas sometimes got him into trouble. Still, she knew the trip was important to the Blueberries, so she finally agreed.

The Blueberries cheered. They couldn't wait to go!

Dot and the rest of the Blueberries met Flik the very next morning. They were ready to begin their journey.

"Look, everyone," said Flik. "I've created a raft to get us to Clover Hill."

The Blueberries put on life preservers and eagerly got into the raft. Soon they were on their way. After a while, Dot saw rapids ahead. "How do we steer this thing?" she asked Flik.

"Steer?" said Flik. "Well, I'm glad you asked!"

He picked up a twig and put one end in the water. Then he began to move the boat with it.

"Wow, Flik! You think of everything!" said Dot, smiling.

Before long, they'd arrived at Clover Hill.

As soon as they got to shore, the Blueberry troop found a safe place to camp. Then they looked for food. When they had gathered some fruit and seeds, Flik examined the food they had found.

"Not everything in nature is good for you—like those berries you're about to eat," Flik said. "They are spicy and hot, hot, hot!"

Luckily, Dot had found some raspberries and Flik had found some sunflower seeds. They sat down and began to eat. "This is fun,"Dot said. "I'm glad we came."

Suddenly, Aphie started to make a lot of noise.

"What's wrong, Aphie?" the princess asked. She whistled, and he came running. The other Blueberries looked around, but they didn't see anything unusual.

"I'm sure it's nothing," said Dot. "He probably just misses my mom."

"Let's go look for more raspberries," Teeny suggested.

"Okay," said Flik, "but first we should hide our stuff. We can leave Aphie behind to guard it." When the ants had hidden everything, Dot gave Aphie a hug. "We'll be back soon," she told him.

The Blueberries didn't know it, but at that very moment, the grasshoppers were approaching! That's what Aphie had been trying to tell them. The grasshoppers were scary creatures. Hopper, his brother Molt, and their friend Thumper were flying over the forest.

"Hey!" cried Molt. "I see a good place to land!"

He led the others to the exact spot the Blueberries had chosen as their campsite!

"Look what I found!" called Molt just after they landed. He held up Aphie.

"I'm not interested in a little aphid!" snapped Hopper.

But Molt thought the aphid was cute. He quickly trapped Aphie under a nutshell. Then he and Thumper set off to search for food for Hopper.

Near the berry patch, Flik looked up at the sun. "It's getting late," he said. "We should head back."

But just before they reached their campsite, Flik and the Blueberries stopped short. There were tracks in the dirt.

"Grasshoppers!" Flik exclaimed. "Maybe we should go home."

As the Blueberries were about to head back to the ant colony, Dot stopped them. "Hey!" she cried. "What about Aphie?"

Flik crawled over to some bushes and peeked at their campsite. Hopper was napping in the very spot where Dot had left Aphie! It was too dangerous to go get him.

But then Flik saw a nutshell hopping across the ground. *Aphie must be underneath the shell*, he thought.

Flik reported back to the troop.

"How can we save Aphie?" asked Dot.

"Well, we've got something the grasshoppers don't," Flik said. "We have big ideas." Then he gathered the girls together to make a plan.

A little while later, Molt and Thumper returned to the campsite with some food. After eating, Molt went to play with his new pet.

But when Molt lifted the nutshell, Aphie heard a noise. It was Dot's whistle. The grasshopper didn't know what it was, but Aphie did! The aphid ran away from Molt as fast as his little legs could carry him.

As soon as Aphie was safe, Flik and the Blueberries started to roll rocks down the hill. The rocks slammed into more rocks. Before long, dozens of them were headed right at Molt! The rocks hit him one after another—*bam! bam! bam!*—and knocked him over.

"Whoa!" he cried.

Molt slowly pulled himself out from under the rocks.

But soon Molt saw a sign that said FREE BERRIES—REALLY TASTY! He scooped up a bunch and took them to his brother. The grasshoppers bit right into them.

"*Aaaaahh!*" they all screamed. The berries were the superhot ones Flik had warned the girls about!

The grasshoppers ran to the river and plunged their heads in, slurping the cool water.

Meanwhile, Flik, the Blueberries, and Aphie decided to sneak out of their hiding place and head back to Ant Island.

Back at home, Dot and the Blueberries told the Queen about their adventure.

"You should have seen them dive for the water, Mom!" Dot said with a giggle.

The Queen was relieved that everyone was safe. She even congratulated Dot and Flik on their quick thinking.

"It just goes to show you,"
said Flik, "a few big ideas
can go a long way!"

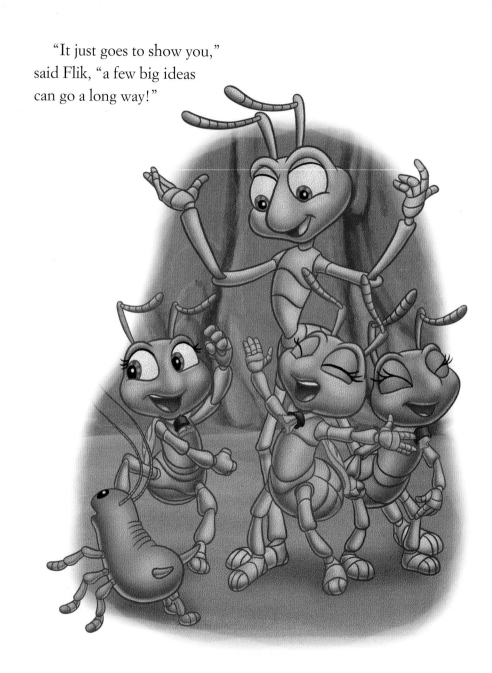